# The Mahatma and

## Henry Rider H

# Table of Contents

# About Haggard:

Henry Rider Haggard was born at Bradenham, Norfolk, to Sir William Meybohm Rider Haggard, a barrister, and Ella Doveton, an author and poet. He was the eighth of ten children. He was initially sent to Garsington Rectory in Oxfordshire to study under the Reverend H.J. Graham but, unlike his older brothers who graduated from various Public Schools, he ended up attending Ipswich Grammar School. This was because his father, who regarded him as somebody who was not going to amount to much, could no longer afford to maintain his expensive private education. After failing his army entrance exam he was sent to a private 'crammer' in London to prepare for the entrance exam for the British Foreign Office, which in the end he never sat. Instead Haggard's father sent him to Africa in an unpaid position as assistant to the secretary to the Lieutenant-Governor of Natal, Sir Henry Bulwer. It was in this role that Haggard was present in Pretoria for the official announcement of the British annexation of the Boer Republic of the Transvaal. In fact, Haggard raised the Union Flag and was forced to read out much of the proclamation following the loss of voice of the official originally entrusted with the duty. As a young man, Haggard fell deeply in love with Lilith Jackson, whom he intended to marry once he obtained paid employment in South Africa. In 1878 he became Registrar of the High Court in the Transvaal, but when he sent his father a letter telling him that he intended to return to England in order to marry Lilith Jackson his father replied that he forbade it until he had made a career for himself. In 1879 he heard that Lilith had married someone else. When he eventually returned to England he married a friend of his sister, Mariana Louisa Margitson and brought her back to Africa. Later they had a son named Jock (who died of measles at the age of 10) and three daughters. Returning again to England in 1882, the couple settled in Ditchingham, Norfolk. Later he lived in Kessingland and had connections with the church in Bungay, Suffolk. He turned to the study of law and was called to the bar in 1884. His practice of law was somewhat desultory, and much of his time was taken up by the writing of novels. Heavily influenced by the larger-than-life adventurers he met in Colonial Africa, most notably Frederick Selous and Frederick Russell Burnham, the great mineral wealth discovered in Africa, and the ruins of ancient lost civilizations in Africa such as Great Zimbabwe, Haggard created his Allan Quatermain adventures. Three of his books, The Wizard (1896), Elissa; the doom of Zimbabwe (1899), and Black Heart and White Heart; a Zulu idyll (1900) are dedicated to Burnham's daughter, Nada, the first white child born in Bulawayo, herself named after Haggard's 1892 book: Nada the Lily. Years later, when Haggard was a successful novelist, he was contacted by his former love, Lilith Jackson. She had been deserted by her husband, who had left her penniless and infected her with syphilis, from which she eventually died. It was Haggard who paid her medical bills. These details were not generally known until the publication of Haggard's 1983 biography by D. S. Higgins. Haggard was heavily involved in agricultural reform and was a member of many Commissions on land use and related affairs, work that involved several trips to the Colonies and Dominions. He was made a Knight Bachelor in 1912, and a Knight Commander of the Order of the British Empire in 1919. He stood unsuccessfully for parliament as a candidate for the Conservative Party.

"Ultimately a good hare was found which took the field at ... There the hounds pressed her, and on the hunt arriving at the edge of the cliff the hare could be seen crossing the beach and going right out to sea. A boat was procured, and the master and some others rowed out to her just as she drowned, and, bringing the body in, gave it to the hounds. A hare swimming out to sea is a sight not often witnessed."—*Local paper, January* 1911.

"... A long check occurred in the latter part of this hunt, the hare having laid up in a hedgerow, from which she was at last evicted by a crack of the whip. Her next place of refuge was a horse-pond, which she tried to swim, but got stuck in the ice midway, and was sinking, when the huntsman went in after her. It was a novel sight to see huntsman and hare being lifted over a wall out of the pond, the eager pack waiting for their prey behind the wall."—*Local paper, February* 1911.

The author supposes that the first of the above extracts must have impressed him. At any rate, on the night after the reading of it, just as he went to sleep, or on the following morning just as he awoke, he cannot tell which, there came to him the title and the outlines of this fantasy, including the command with which it ends. With a particular clearness did he seem to see the picture of the Great White Road, "straight as the way of the Spirit, and broad as the breast of Death," and of the little Hare travelling towards the awful Gates.

Like the Mahatma of this fable, he expresses no opinion as to the merits of the controversy between the Red-faced Man and the Hare that, without search on his own part, presented itself to his mind in so odd a fashion. It is one on which anybody interested in such matters can form an individual judgment.

## 1 The Mahatma

Mahatma, "great-souled." "One of a class of persons with preter- natural powers, imagined to exist in India and Thibet."—*New English Dictionary*.

Everyone has seen a hare, either crouched or running in the fields, or hanging dead in a poulterer's shop, or lastly pathetic, even dreadful- looking and in this form almost indistinguishable from a skinned cat, on the domestic table. But not many people have met a Mahatma, at least to their knowledge. Not many people know even who or what a Mahatma is. The majority of those who chance to have heard the title are apt to confuse it with another, that of Mad Hatter.

This is even done of malice prepense (especially, for obvious reasons, if a hare is in any way concerned) in scorn, not in ignorance, by persons who are well acquainted with the real meaning of the word and even with its Sanscrit origin. The truth is that an incredulous Western world puts no faith in Mahatmas. To it a Mahatma is a kind of spiritual Mrs. Harris, giving an address in Thibet at which no letters are delivered. Either, it says, there is no such person, or he is a fraudulent scamp with no greater occult powers—well, than a hare.

I confess that this view of Mahatmas is one that does not surprise me in the least. I never met, and I scarcely expect to meet, an individual entitled to set "Mahatma" after his name. Certainly *I* have no right to do so, who only took that title on the spur of the moment when the Hare asked me how I was called, and now make use of it as a *nom-de-plume*. It is true there is Jorsen, by whose order, for it amounts to that, I publish this history. For aught I know Jorsen may be a Mahatma, but he does not in the least look the part.

Imagine a bluff person with a strong, hard face, piercing grey eyes, and very prominent, bushy eyebrows, of about fifty or sixty years of age. Add a Scotch accent and a meerschaum pipe, which he smokes even when he is wearing a frock coat and a tall hat, and you have Jorsen. I believe that he lives somewhere in the country, is well off, and practises gardening. If so he has never asked me to his place, and I only meet him when he comes to Town, as I understand, to visit flower- shows.

Then I always meet him because he orders me to do so, not

by letter or by word of mouth but in quite a different way. Suddenly I receive an impression in my mind that I am to go to a certain place at a certain hour, and that there I shall find Jorsen. I do go, sometimes to an hotel, sometimes to a lodging, sometimes to a railway station or to the corner of a particular street and there I do find Jorsen smoking his big meerschaum pipe. We shake hands and he explains why he has sent for me, after which we talk of various things. Never mind what they are, for that would be telling Jorsen's secrets as well as my own, which I must not do.

It may be asked how I came to know Jorsen. Well, in a strange way. Nearly thirty years ago a dreadful thing happened to me. I was married and, although still young, a person of some mark in literature. Indeed even now one or two of the books which I wrote are read and remembered, although it is supposed that their author has long left the world.

The thing which happened was that my wife and our daughter were coming over from the Channel Islands, where they had been on a visit (she was a Jersey woman), and, and —well, the ship was lost, that's all. The shock broke my heart, in such a way that it has never been mended again, but unfortunately did not kill me.

Afterwards I took to drink and sank, as drunkards do. Then the river began to draw me. I had a lodging in a poor street at Chelsea, and I could hear the river calling me at night, and—I wished to die as the others had died. At last I yielded, for the drink had rotted out all my moral sense. About one o'clock of a wild, winter morning I went to a bridge I knew where in those days policemen rarely came, and listened to that call of the water.

"Come!" it seemed to say. "This world is the real hell, ending in the eternal naught. The dreams of a life beyond and of re-union there are but a demon's mocking breathed into the mortal heart, lest by its universal suicide mankind should rob him of his torture-pit. There is no truth in all your father taught you" (he was a clergyman and rather eminent in his profession), "there is no hope for man, there is nothing he can win except the deep happiness of sleep. Come and sleep."

Such were the arguments of that Voice of the river, the old, familiar arguments of desolation and despair. I leant over the parapet; in another moment I should have been gone, when I became aware that some one was standing near to me. I did not see the person because it was too dark. I did not hear him because of the raving of the wind. But I knew that he was there. So I waited until the moon shone out for a while between the edges of two ragged clouds, the shapes of which I can see to this hour. It showed me Jorsen, looking just as he does to-day, for he never seems to change— Jorsen, on whom, to my knowledge, I had not set eyes before.

"Even a year ago," he said, in his strong, rough voice, "you would not have allowed your mind to be convinced by such arguments as those which you have just heard in the Voice of the river. That is one of the worst sides of drink; it decays the reason as it does the body. You must have noticed it yourself."

I replied that I had, for I was surprised into acquiescence. Then I grew defiant and asked him what he knew of the arguments which were or were not influencing me. To my surprise—no, that is not the word—to my bewilderment, he repeated them to me one by one just as they had arisen a few minutes before in my heart. Moreover, he told me what I had been about to do, and why I was about to do it.

"You know me and my story," I muttered at last.

"No," he answered, "at least not more than I know that of many men with whom I chance to be in touch. That is, I have not met you for nearly eleven hundred years. A thousand and eighty-six, to be correct. I was a blind priest then and you were the captain of Irene's guard."

At this news I burst out laughing and the laugh did me good. "I did not know I was so old," I said.

"Do you call that old?" answered Jorsen. "Why, the first time that we had anything to do with each other, so far as I can learn, that is, was over eight thousand years ago, in Egypt before the beginning of recorded history."

"I thought that I was mad, but you are madder," I said.

"Doubtless. Well, I am so mad that I managed to be here in time to save you from suicide, as once in the past you saved me, for thus things come round. But your rooms are near, are they not? Let us go there and talk. This place is cold and the river is always calling."

That was how I came to know Jorsen, whom I believe to be one of the greatest men alive. On this particular night that I have described he told me many things, and since then he has taught me much, me and a few others. But whether he is what is called a Mahatma I am sure I do not know. He has never claimed such a rank in my hearing, or indeed to be anything more than a man who has succeeded in winning a knowledge of his own powers out of the depths of the dark that lies behind us. Of course I mean out of his past in other incarnations long before he was Jorsen. Moreover, by degrees, as I grew fit to bear the light, he showed me something of my own, and of how the two were intertwined. But all these things are secrets of which I have perhaps no right to speak at present. It is enough to say that Jorsen changed the current of my life on that night when he saved me from death.

For instance, from that day onwards to the present time I have never touched the drink which so nearly ruined me. Also the darkness has rolled away, and with it every doubt and fear; I know the truth, and for that truth I live. Considered from certain aspects such knowledge, I admit, is not altogether desirable. Thus it has deprived me of my interest in earthly things. Ambition has left me altogether; for years I have had no wish to succeed in the profession which I adopted in my youth, or in any other. Indeed I doubt whether the elements of worldly success still remain in me; whether they are not entirely burnt away by that fire of wisdom in which I have bathed. How can we strive to win a crown we have no longer any desire to wear? Now I desire other crowns and at times I wear them, if only for a little while. My spirit grows and grows. It is dragging at its strings.

What am I to look at? A small, white-haired man with a thin and rather plaintive face in which are set two large, dark eyes that continually seem to soften and develop. That is my picture. And what am I in the world? I will tell you. On certain days of the week I employ myself in editing a trade journal that has to do with haberdashery. On another day I act as auctioneer to a firm which imports and sells cheap Italian statuary; modern, very modern copies of the antique, florid marble vases, and so forth. Some of you who read may have passed such marts in different parts of the city, or even have dropped in and purchased a bust or a tazza for a surprisingly small sum. Perhaps I knocked it down to you, only too pleased to find a *bonâ fide* bidder amongst my company.

As for the rest of my time—well, I employ it in doing what good I can among the poor and those who need comfort or who are bereaved, especially among those who are bereaved, for to such I am sometimes able to bring the breath of hope that blows from another shore.

Occasionally also I amuse myself in my own fashion. Thus sure knowledge has come to me about certain epochs in the past in which I lived in other shapes, and I study those epochs, hoping that one day I may find time to write of them and of the parts I played in them. Some of these parts are extremely interesting, especially as I am of course able to contrast them with our modern modes of thought and action.

They do not all come back to me with equal clearness, the earlier lives being, as one might expect, the more difficult to recover and the comparatively recent ones the easiest. Also they seem to range over a vast stretch of time, back indeed to the days of primeval, prehistoric man. In short, I think the subconscious in some ways resembles the conscious and natural memory; that which is very far off to it grows dim and blurred, that which is comparatively close remains clear and sharp, although of course this rule is not invariable. Moreover there is foresight as well as memory. At least from time to time I seem to come in touch with future events and states of society in which I shall have my share.

I believe some thinkers hold a theory that such conditions as those of past, present, and future do not in fact exist; that everything already is, standing like a completed column between earth and heaven; that the sum is added up, the equation worked out. At times I am tempted to believe in the truth of this proposition. But if it be true, of course it remains difficult to obtain a clear view of other parts of the column than that in which we happen to find ourselves objectively conscious at any given period, and needless to say impossible to see it from base to capital.

However this may be, no individual entity pervades all the column. There are great sections of it with which that entity has nothing to do, although it always seems to appear again above. I suppose that those sections which are empty of an individual and his atmosphere represent the intervals between his lives which he spends in sleep, or in states of existence with which this world is not concerned, but of such gulfs of oblivion and states of being I know nothing.

To take a single instance of what I do know: once this spirit of mine, that now by the workings of destiny for a little while occupies the body of a fourth-rate auctioneer, and of the editor of a trade journal, dwelt in that of a Pharaoh of Egypt —never mind which Pharoah. Yes, although you may laugh and think me mad to say it, for me the legions fought and thundered; to me the peoples bowed and the secret sanctuaries were opened that I and I alone might commune with the gods; I who in the flesh and after it myself was worshipped as a god.

Well, of this forgotten Royalty of whom little is known save what a few inscriptions have to tell, there remains a portrait statue in the British Museum. Sometimes I go to look at that statue and try to recall exactly under what circumstances I caused it to be shaped, puzzling out the story bit by bit.

Not long ago I stood thus absorbed and did not notice that the hour of the closing of the great gallery had come. Still I stood and gazed and dreamt till the policeman on duty, seeing and suspecting me, came up and roughly ordered me to begone.

The man's tone angered me. I laid my hand on the foot of the statue, for it had just come back to me that it was a "Ka" image, a sacred thing, any Egyptologist will know what I mean, which for ages had sat in a chamber of my tomb. Then the Ka that clings to it eternally awoke at my touch and knew me, or so I suppose. At least I felt myself change. A new strength came into me; my shape, battered in this world's storms, put on something of its ancient dignity; my eyes grew royal. I looked at that man as Pharaoh may have looked at one who had done him insult. He saw the change and trembled—yes, trembled. I believe he thought I was some imperial ghost that the shadows of evening had caused him to mistake for man; at any rate he gasped out—

"I beg your pardon, I was obeying orders. I hope your Majesty won't hurt me. Now I think of it I have been told that things come out of these old statues in the night."

Then turning he ran, literally ran, where to I am sure I do not know, probably to seek the fellowship of some other policeman. In due course I followed, and, lifting the bar at the end of the hall, departed without further question asked. Afterwards I was very glad to think that I had done the man no injury. At the moment I knew that I could hurt him if I would, and what is more I had the desire to do so. It came to me, I suppose, with that breath of the past when I was so great and absolute. Perhaps I, or that part of me then incarnate, was a tyrant in those days, and this is why now I must be so humble. Fate is turning my pride to its hammer and beating it out of me.

For thus in the long history of the soul it serves all our vices.

## 2 The Great White Road

Now, as I have hinted, under the teaching of Jorsen, who saved me from degradation and self-murder, yes, and helped me with money until once again I could earn a livelihood, I have acquired certain knowledge and wisdom of a sort that are not common. That is, Jorsen taught me the elements of these things; he set my feet upon the path which thenceforward, having the sight, I have been able to follow for myself. How I followed it does not matter, nor could I teach others if I would.

I am no member of any mystic brotherhood, and, as I have explained, no Mahatma, although I have called myself thus for present purposes because the name is a convenient cloak. I repeat that I am ignorant if there are such people as Mahatmas, though if so I think Jorsen must be one of them. Still he never told me this. What he has told is that every individual spirit must work out its own destiny quite independently of others. Indeed, being rather fond of fine phrases, he has sometimes spoken to me of, or rather, insisted upon what he called "the lonesome splendour of the human soul," which it is our business to perfect through various lives till I can scarcely appreciate and am certainly unable to describe.

To tell the truth, the thought of this "lonesome splendour" to which it seems some of us may attain, alarms me. I have had enough of being lonesome, and I do not ask for any particular splendour. My only ambitions are to find those whom I have lost, and in whatever life I live to be of use to others. However, as I gather that the exalted condition to which Jorsen alludes is thousands of ages off for any of us, and may after all mean something quite different to what it seems to mean, the thought of it does not trouble me over much. Meanwhile what I seek is the vision of those I love.

Now I have this power. Occasionally when I am in deep sleep some part of me seems to leave my body and to be transported quite outside the world. It travels, as though I were already dead, to the Gates that all who live must pass, and there takes its stand, on the Great White Road, watching those who have been called speed by continually. Those upon the earth know nothing of that Road. Blinded by their pomps and vanities, they cannot see, they will not see it always growing towards the feet of every one of them. But I see and know. Of course you who read will say that this is but a dream of mine, and it may be. Still, if so, it is a very wonderful dream, and except for the change of the passing people, or rather of those who have been people, always very much the same.

There, straight as the way of the Spirit and broad as the breast of Death, is the Great White Road running I know not whence, up to those Gates that gleam like moonlight and are higher than the Alps. There beyond the Gates the radiant Presences move mysteriously. Thence at the appointed time the Voice cries and they are opened with a sound like to that of deepest thunder, or sometimes are burned away, while from the Glory that lies beyond flow the sweet-faced welcomers to greet those for whom they wait, bearing the cups from which they give to drink. I do not know what is in the cups, whether it be a draught of Lethe or some baptismal water of new birth, or both; but always the thirsting, world-worn soul appears to change, and then as it were to be lost in the Presence that gave the cup. At least they are lost to my sight. I see them no more.

Why do I watch those Gates, in truth or in dream, before my time? Oh! You can guess. That perchance I may behold those for whom my heart burns with a quenchless, eating fire. And once I beheld—not the mother but the child, my child, changed indeed, mysterious, wonderful, gleaming like a star, with eyes so deep that in their depths my humanity seemed to swoon.

She came forward; she knew me; she smiled and laid her finger on her lips. She shook her hair about her and in it vanished as in a cloud. Yet as she vanished a voice spoke in my heart, her voice, and the words it said were—

"Wait, our Beloved! Wait!"

Mark well. "Our Beloved," not "My Beloved." So there are others by whom I am beloved, or at least one other, and I know well who that one must be.

After this dream, perhaps I had better call it a dream, I was ill for a long while, for the joy and the glory of it overpowered me and brought me near to the death I had always sought. But I recovered, for my hour is not yet. Moreover, for a long while as we reckon time, some years indeed, I obeyed the injunction and sought the Great White Road no more. At length the longing grew too strong for me and I returned thither, but never again did the vision come. Its word was spoken, its mission was fulfilled. Yet from time to time I, a mortal, seem to stand upon the borders of that immortal Road and watch the newly dead who travel it towards the glorious Gates.

Once or twice there have been among them people whom I have known. As these pass me I appear to have the power of looking into their hearts, and there I read strange things. Sometimes they are beautiful things and sometimes ugly things. Thus I have learned that those I thought bad were really good in the main, for who can claim to be quite good? And on the other hand that those I believed to be as honest as the day —well, had their faults.

To take an example which I quote because it is so absurd. The rooms I live in were owned by a prim old woman who for more than twenty years was my landlady. She and I were great friends, indeed she tended me like a mother, and when I was so ill nursed me as perhaps few mothers would have done. Yet while I was watching on the Road suddenly she came by, and with horror I saw that during all those years she had been robbing me, taking, I am sorry to say, many things, in money, trinkets, and food. Often I had discussed with her where these articles could possibly have gone, till finally suspicion settled upon the man who cleaned the windows. Yes, and worst of all, he was prosecuted, and I gave evidence against him, or rather strengthened her evidence, on faith of which the magistrate sent him to prison for a month.

"Oh! Mrs Smithers," I said to her, "how *could* you do it, Mrs. Smithers?"

She stopped and looked about her terrified, so that my heart smote me and I added in haste, "Don't be frightened, Mrs. Smithers; I forgive you."

"I can't see you, sir," she exclaimed, or so I dreamed, "but there! I always knew you would."

"Yes, Mrs. Smithers," I replied; "but how about the window-cleaner who went to jail and lost his situation?"

Then she passed on or was drawn away without making any answer.

Now comes the odd part of the story. When I woke up on the following morning in my rooms, it was to be informed by the frightened maid-of- all-work that Mrs. Smithers had been found dead in her bed. Moreover, a few days later I learned from a lawyer that she had made a will leaving me everything she possessed, including the lease of her house and nearly £1000, for she had been a saving old person during all her long life.

Well, I sought out that window-cleaner and compensated him handsomely, saying that I had found I was mistaken in the evidence I gave against him. The rest of the property I kept, and I hope that it was not wrong of me to do so. It will be remembered that some of it was already my own, temporarily diverted into another channel, and for the rest I have so many to help. To be frank I do not spend much upon myself.

## 3 The Hare

Now I have done with myself, or rather with my own insignificant present history, and come to that of the Hare. It impressed me a good deal at the time, which is not long ago, so much indeed that I communicated the facts to Jorsen. He ordered me to publish them, and what Jorsen orders must be done. I don't know why this should be, but it is so. He has authority of a sort that I am unable to define.

One night after the usual aspirations and concentration of mind, which by the way are not always successful, I passed into what occultists call spirit, and others a state of dream. At any rate I found myself upon the borders of the Great White Road, as near to the mighty Gates as I am ever allowed to come. How far that may be away I cannot tell. Perhaps it is but a few yards and perhaps it is the width of this great world, for in that place which my spirit visits time and distance do not exist. There all things are new and strange, not to be reckoned by our measures. There the sight is not our sight nor the hearing our hearing. I repeat that all things are different, but that difference I cannot describe, and if I could it would prove past comprehension.

There I sat by the borders of the Great White Road, my eyes fixed upon the Gates above which the towers mount for miles on miles, outlined against an encircling gloom with the radiance of the world beyond the worlds. Four-square they stand, those towers, and fourfold the gates that open to the denizens of other earths. But of these I have no knowledge beyond the fact that it is so in my visions.

I sat upon the borders of the Road, my eyes fixed in hope upon the Gates, though well I knew that the hope would never be fulfilled, and watched the dead go by.

They were many that night. Some plague was working in the East and unchaining thousands. The folk that it loosed were strange to me who in this particular life have seldom left England, and I studied them with curiosity; high-featured, dark-hued people with a patient air. The knowledge which I have told me that one and all they were very ancient souls who often and often had walked this Road before, and therefore, although as yet they did not know it, were well accustomed to the journey. No, I am wrong, for here and there an individual did know. Indeed one deep-eyed, wistful little woman, who carried a baby in her arms, stopped for a moment and spoke to me.

"The others cannot see you as I do," she said. "Priest of the Queen of queens, I know you well; hand in hand we climbed by the seven stairways to the altars of the moon."

"Who is the Queen of queens?" I asked.

"Have you forgotten her of the hundred names whose veils we lifted one by one; her whose breast was beauty and whose eyes were truth? In a day to come you will remember. Farewell till we walk this Road no more."

"Stay—when did we meet?"

"When our souls were young," she answered, and faded from my ken like a shadow from the sea.

After the Easterns came many others from all parts of the earth. Then suddenly appeared a company of about six hundred folk of every age and English in their looks. They were not so calm as are the majority of those who make this journey. When I read the papers a few days later I understood why. A great passenger ship had sunk suddenly in mid ocean and they were all cut off unprepared.

When, followed by a few stragglers, these had passed and gathered themselves in the red shadow beneath the gateway towers waiting for the summons, an unusual thing occurred. For a few moments the Road was left quite empty. After that last great stroke Death seemed to be resting on his laurels. When thus unpeopled it looked a very vast place like to a huge arched causeway, bordered on either side by blackness, but itself gleaming with a curious phosphorescence such as once or twice I have seen in the waters of a summer sea at night.

Presently in the very centre of this illuminated desolation, whilst it was as yet far away, something caught my eye, something so strange to the place, so utterly unfamiliar that I watched it earnestly, wondering what it might be. Nearer and nearer it came, with curious, uncertain hops; yes, a little brown object that hopped.

"Well," I said to myself, "if I were not where I am I should say that yonder thing was a hare. Only what would a hare be doing on the Great White Road? How could a hare tread the pathway of eternal souls? I must be mistaken."

So I reflected whilst still the thing hopped on, until I became certain that either I suffered from delusions, or that it was a hare; indeed a particularly fine hare, much such a one as a friend of my old landlady, Mrs. Smithers, had once sent her as a Christmas present from Norfolk, which hare I ate.

A few more hops brought it opposite to my post of observation. Here it halted as though it seemed to see me. At any rate it sat up in the alert fashion that hares have, its forepaws hanging absurdly in front of it, with one ear, on which there was a grey blotch, cocked and one dragging, and sniffed with its funny little nostrils. Then it began to talk to me. I do not mean that it really talked, but the thoughts which were in its mind were flashed on to my mind so that I understood perfectly, yes, and could answer them in the same fashion. It said, or thought, thus:—

"You are real. You are a man who yet lives beneath the sun, though how you came here I do not know. I hate men, all hares do, for men are cruel to them. Still it is a comfort in this strange place to see something one has seen before and to be able to talk even to a man, which I could never do until the change came, the dreadful change—I mean because of the way of it," and it seemed to shiver. "May I ask you some questions?"

"Certainly," I said or rather thought back.

"You are sure that they won't make you angry so that you hurt me?"

"I can't hurt you, even if I wished to do so. You are not a hare any longer, if you ever were one, but only the shadow of a hare."

"Ah! I thought as much, and that's a good thing anyhow. Tell me, Man, have you ever been torn to pieces by dogs?"

"Good gracious! no."

"Or coursed, or hunted, or caught in a trap, or shot all over your back, or twisted up in nets and choked in snares? Or have you swum out to sea to die more easily, or seen your mate and mother and father killed?"

"No, no. Please stop, Hare; your questions are very

unpleasant."

"Not half so unpleasant as the things are themselves, I can assure you, Man. I will tell you my story if you like; then you can judge for yourself. But first, if you will, do you tell me why I am here. Have you seen more hares about this place?"

"Never, nor any other animals. No, I am wrong, once I saw a dog."

The Hare looked about it anxiously.

"A dog. How horrible! What was it doing? Hunting? If there are no hares here what could it be hunting? A rabbit, or a pheasant with a broken wing, or perhaps a fox? I should not mind so much if it were a fox. I hate foxes; they catch young hares when they are asleep and eat them."

"None of these things. I was told that it belonged to a little girl who died. That broke its heart, so that it died also when they shut her up in a box. Therefore it was allowed to accompany her here because it had loved so much. Indeed I saw them together, both very happy, and together they went through those gates."

"If dogs love little girls why don't they love hares, at least as anything likes to be loved, for the dog didn't want to eat the little girl, did it? I see you can't answer me. Now would you like me to tell you my story? Something inside of me is saying that I am to do so if you will listen; also that there is plenty of time, for I am not wanted at present, and when I am I can run to those gates much quicker than you could."

"I should like it very much, Hare. Once a prophet heard an ass speak in order to warn him. But since then, except very, very rarely in dreams, no creature has talked to a man, so far as I know. Perhaps you wish to warn me about something, or others through me, as the ass warned Balaam."

"Who is Balaam? I never heard of Balaam. He wasn't the man who fetches dead pheasants in the donkey-cart, was he? If so, I've seen him make the ass talk—with a thick stick. No? Well, never mind, I daresay I should not understand about him if you told me. Now for my story."

Then the Hare sat itself down, planting its forepaws firmly in front of it, as these animals do when they are on the watch, looked up at me and began to pour the contents of its mind into mine.

I was born, it said, or rather told me by thought transference, in a field of growing corn near to a big wood. At least I suppose I was born there, though the first thing I remember is playing about in the wheat with two other little ones of my own size, a brother and a sister that were born with me. It was at night, for a great, round, shining thing which I now know was the moon, hung in the sky above us. We gambolled together and were very happy, till presently my mother came—I remember how big she looked—and cuffed me with her paw because I had led the others away from the place where she had told us to stop, and given her a great hunt to find us. That is the first thing I remember about my mother. Afterwards she seemed sorry because she had hurt me, and nursed us all three, letting me have the most milk. My mother always loved me the best of us, because I was such a fine leveret, with a pretty grey patch on my left ear. Just as I had finished drinking another hare came who was my father. He was very large, with a glossy coat and big shining eyes that always seemed to see everything, even when it was behind him.

He was frightened about something, and hustled my mother and us little ones out of the wheat-field into the big wood by which it is bordered. As we left the field I saw two tall creatures that afterwards I came to know were men. They were placing wire-netting round the field—you see I understand now what all these things were, although of course I did not at the time. The two ends of the wire netting had nearly come together. There was only a little gap left through which we could run. Another young hare, or it may have been a rabbit, had got entangled in it, and one of the men was beating it to death with a stick. I remember that the sound of its screams made me feel cold down the back, for I had never heard anything like that before, and this was the first that I had seen of pain and death.

The other man saw us slipping through and ran at us with his stick. My mother went first and escaped him. Then came my sister, then I, then my brother. My father was last of all. The man hit with his stick and it came down thud along side of me, just touching my fur. He hit again and broke the foreleg of my brother. Still we all managed to get through into the wood, except my father who was behind.

"There's the old buck!" cried one of the men (I understand what he said now, though at the time it meant nothing to me). "Knock him on the head!"

So leaving us alone they ran at him. But my father was much too quick for them. He rushed back into the corn and afterwards joined us in the wood, for he had seen wire before and knew how to escape it. Still he was terribly frightened and made us keep in the wood till the following evening, not even allowing my mother to go to her form in the rough pasture on its other side and lie up there.

Also we were in trouble because my brother's forepaw was broken. It gave him a great deal of pain, so that he could not rest or sleep. After a while, however, it mended up in a fashion, but he was never able to run as fast as we could, nor did he grow so big. In the end the mother fox killed him, as I shall tell.

My mother asked my father what the men with the sticks were doing— for, you know, many animals can talk to each other in their own way, even if they are of different kinds. He told her that they were protecting the wheat to prevent us from eating it, to which she answered angrily that hares must live somehow, especially when they had young ones to nurse. My father replied that men did not seem to think so, and perhaps they had young ones also. I see now that my father was a philosophic hare. But are you tired of my story?

"Not at all," I answered; "go on, please. It is very interesting to hear things described from the animal's point of view, especially when that animal has grown wise and learned to understand."

"Ah," answered the Hare. "I see what you mean. And it is odd, but I do understand. All has become clear to me. I don't know what happened when I died, but there came a change, and I knew that I who was but a beast always have been and still am a necessary part of everything as much as you are, though more helpless and humble. Yes, I am as ancient and as far-reaching as yourself, but how I began and how I shall end is dark to me. Well, I will go on with my story.

It must have been a moon or so later, after my mother had

given up nursing me, that I went to lie out by myself. There was a big house on the hillside overlooking the sea, and near to it were gardens surrounded by a wall. Also outside of this wall was another patch of garden where cabbages grew. I found a way to those cabbages and kept it secret, for I was greedy and wanted them all for myself. I used to creep in at night and eat them, also some flowers with spiky leaves that grew round them which had a very fine flavour. Then after the dawn came I went to a form which I had made under a furze bush on the slope that ran down to the sea, and slept there.

One day I was awakened by something white, hard, and round which rolled gently and stopped still quite close to me. It was not alive, although it had a queer smell, and I wondered why it moved at all. Presently I heard voices and there appeared a little man, and with him somebody who was not a man because it was differently dressed and spoke in a higher voice. I saw that they had sticks in their hands and thought of running away, then that it would be safer to lie quite close. They came up to me and the little man said—

"There's the ball; pick it up, Ella, the lie is too bad."

She, for now I know it was what is called a girl, stooped to obey and saw my back.

"Tom," she said in a whisper, "here's a young hare on its form."

"Get out of the light," he answered, "and I'll kill it," and he lifted the stick he held, which had a twisted iron end.

"No," she said, "catch it alive; I want a hare to be a friend to my rabbit, which has lost all its little ones."

"Lost them? Eaten them, you mean, because you would

always go and stare at it," said Tom. "Where's the leveret? Oh! I see. Now, look out!"

A moment later and I was in darkness. Tom had thrown himself upon the top of me and was grabbing at me with his hands. I nearly got away, but as my head poked up under his arm the girl caught hold of it.

"Oh! it's scratching," she cried, as indeed I was with all my might. "Hold it, Tom, hold it!"

"Hold it yourself," said Tom, "my face is full of furze prickles." So she held and presently he helped her, till in the end I was tied up in a pocket-handkerchief and carried I knew not whither. Indeed I was almost mad with fear.

When I came to myself I found that I was within a kind of wire run which smelt foully, as though hundreds of things had lived in it for years. There was a hutch at the end of the run in which sat an enormous she-rabbit, quite as big as my mother, a fierce-looking brute with long yellow teeth. I was afraid of that rabbit and got as far from it as I could. Presently it hopped out and looked at me.

"What are you doing here?" it asked. "Can't you talk? Well, it doesn't matter. If I get hungry I'll eat you! Do you hear that? I'll eat you, as I did all the others," and it showed its big yellow teeth and hopped back into the hutch.

After that Tom and the girl came and gave us plenty of food which the big rabbit ate, for I could touch nothing. For two days they came, and then I think they forgot all about us. I grew very hungry, and at night filled myself with some of the remaining food, such as stale cabbage leaves. By next morning all was gone, and the big rabbit grew hungry also. All that day it hopped about sniffing at me and showing its yellow teeth.

"I shall eat you to-night," it said.

I ran round and round the pen in terror, till at last I found a place where rats had been working under the wire, almost big enough for me to squeeze through, but not quite.

The sun went down and the big she-rabbit came out.

"Now I am going to eat you," it said, "as I ate all the others. I am hungry, very hungry," and it prodded me about with its nose and rolled me over.

At last with a little squeal it drove its big yellow teeth into me behind. Oh! how they hurt! I was near the rat-hole. I rushed at it, scrabbling and wriggling. The big rabbit pounced on me with its fore- feet, trying to hold me, but too late, for I was through, leaving some of my fur behind me. I ran, how I ran! without stopping, till at length I found my mother in the rough pasture by the wood and told her everything.

"Ah!" she said, "that's what comes of greediness and of trying to be too clever. Now, perhaps, you will learn to stop at home."

So I did for a long while.

The summer went by without anything particular happening, except that my brother with the lame foot was eaten by the mother fox. That great red beast was always prowling about, and at night surprised us in a field near the wood where we were feeding on some beautiful turnips. The rest of us got away, but my brother being lame, was not quick enough. The fox caught him, and I heard her sharp white teeth crunch into his bones. The sound made me quite sick, and my mother was very sad afterwards. She complained to my father of the cruelty of foxes, but he, who, as I have said, was a philosopher, answered her almost in her own words.

"Foxes must live, and this one has young to feed, and therefore is always hungry. There are three of them in a hole at the top of the wood," he remarked. "Also our son was lame and would certainly have been caught when the hunting begins."

"What's the hunting?" I asked.

"Never mind," said my father sharply. "No doubt you'll find out in time, that is if you live through the shooting."

"What's the shooting?" I began, but my father cuffed me over the head and I was silent.

I may tell you that my mother soon got over the loss of my brother, for just about that time she had four new little ones, after which neither she nor my father seemed to think any more about us. My sister and I hated those little ones. We two alone remembered my brother, and sometimes wondered whether he was quite gone or would one day come back. The fox, I am glad to say, got caught in a trap. At least I am not glad now—I was glad because, you see, I was so much afraid of her.

## 4 The Shooting

I was quite close by one morning when the fox, who was smelling about after me, I suppose because it had liked my brother so much, got caught in the big trap which was covered over artfully with earth and baited with some stuff which stank horribly. I remember it looked very like my own hind-legs. The fox, not being able to find me, went to this filth and tried to eat it.

Then suddenly there was a dreadful fuss. The fox yelped and flew into the air. I saw that a great black thing was fast on its forepaw. How that fox did jump and roll! It was quite wonderful to see her. She looked like a great yellow ball, except for a lot of white marks about the head, which were her teeth. But the trap would not come away, because it was tied to a root with a chain.

At last the fox grew tired and, lying down, began to think, licking its paw as it thought and making a kind of moaning noise. Next it commenced gnawing at the root after trying the chain and finding that its teeth would not go into it. While it was doing this I heard the sound of a man somewhere in the wood. So did the fox, and oh! it looked so frightened. It lay down panting, its tongue hanging out and its ears pressed back against its head, and whisked its big tail from side to side. Then it began to gnaw again, but this time at its own leg. It wanted to bite it off and so get away. I thought this very brave of the fox, and though I hated it because it had eaten my brother and tried to eat me, I felt quite sorry.

It was about half through its leg when the man came. I remember that he had a cat with a little red collar on its neck, and an owl in his hand, both of them dead, for he was Giles, the head-keeper, going round his traps. He was a tall man with sandy whiskers and a rough voice, and he carried a single-barrelled gun under his arm.

You see, now that I am dead I know the use of these things, just as I understand all that was said, though of course at the time it had no meaning for me. Still I find that I have forgotten nothing, not one word from the beginning of my life to the end.

The keeper, who was on his way to the place where he nailed the creatures he did not like by dozens upon poles, looked down and saw the fox. "Oh! my beauty," he said, "so I have got you at last. Don't you think yourself clever trying to bite off that leg. You'd have done it too, only I came along just in time. Well, good night, old girl, you won't have no more of my pheasants."

Then he lifted the gun. There was a most dreadful noise and the fox rolled over and lay still.

"There you are, all neat and tidy, my dear," said the keeper. "Now I must just tuck you away in the hollow tree before old Grampus sneaks round and sees you, for if he should it will be almost as much as my place is worth."

Next he set his foot on the trap and, opening it, took hold of the fox by the fore-legs to carry it off. The cat and the owl he stuffed away into a great pocket in his coat.

"Jemima! don't you wholly stink," he said, then gave a most awful yell.

The fox wasn't quite dead after all, it was only shamming

dead. At any rate it got Giles' hand in its mouth and made its teeth meet through the flesh.

Now the keeper began to jump about just as the fox had done when it set its paw in the trap, shouting and saying all sorts of things that somehow I don't think I ought to repeat here. Round and round he went with the fox hanging to his hand, like hares do when they dance together, for he couldn't get it off anyhow. At last he tumbled down into a pool of mud and water, and when he got up again all wet through I saw that the fox was really dead. But it had died biting, and now I know that this pleased it very much.

It was just then that the man whom the keeper had called Grampus came up. He was a big, fat man with a very red face, who made a kind of blowing noise when he walked fast. I know now that he was the lord of all the other men about that place, that he lived in the house which looked over the sea, and that the boy and girl who put me in with the yellow-toothed rabbit were his children. He was what the farmers called "a first-rate all-round sportsman," which means, my friend—but what is your name?

"Oh! Mahatma," I answered at hazard.

"Which means, my friend Mahatma, that he spent most of the year in killing the lower animals such as me. Yes, he spent quite eight months out of the twelve in killing us one way and another, for when there was no more killing to be done in his own country, he would travel to others and kill there. He would even kill pigeons from a trap, or young rooks just out of their nests, or rats in a stack, or sparrows among ivy, rather than not kill anything. I've heard Giles say so to the under-keeper and call him "a regular slaughterer" and "a true- blood Englishman."

Yet, my friend Mahatma, I say in the light of the truth which has come to me, that according to his knowledge Grampus was a good man. Thus, what little time he had to spare from sport he passed in helping his brother men by sending them to prison. Although of course he never worked or earned anything, he was very rich, because money flowed to him from other people who had been very rich, but who at last were forced to travel this Road and could not bring it with them. If they could have brought it, I am sure that Grampus would never have got any. However, he did get it, and he aided a great many people with that part of it which he found he could not spend upon himself. He was a very good man, only he liked killing us lower creatures, whom he bred up with his money to be killed.

"Go on with your story, Hare," I said; "when I see this Red-faced Man I will judge of him for myself. Probably you are prejudiced about him."

"I daresay I am," answered the Hare, rubbing its nose; "but please observe that I am not speaking unkindly of Grampus, although before I have done you may think that I might have reason to do so. However, you will be able to form your own opinion when he comes here, which I am sure he does not mean to do for many, many years. The world is much too comfortable for him. He does not wish to leave it."

"Still he may be obliged to do so, Hare."

"Oh! no, people like that are never obliged to do anything they do not like. It is only poor things such as you and I, Mahatma, which must suffer. I can see that you have had a great deal to bear, and so have I, for we were born to suffering as the Red-faced Man was born to happiness."

"Go on with your story, Hare," I repeated. "You are becoming metaphysical and therefore dull. The time is short and I want to hear what happened."

"Quite so, Mahatma. Well, Grampus came up breathing very heavily and looking very red in the face. He held his hat in one hand and a large crooked stick in the other, and even the top of his head, on which no hair grew, was red, for he had been running.

"What the deuce is the matter?" he puffed. "Oh! it is you, Giles, is it? What are you doing, sir, looking like that, all covered with blood and mud? Has a poacher shot you, or what?"

"No, Squire," answered Giles humbly, touching his hat. "I have shot a poacher, that's all, and it has given me what for," and he lifted the body of the fox from the water.

"A fox," said Grampus, "a fox! Do you mean to say, Giles, that you have dared to shoot a fox, and a vixen with a litter too? How often have I told you that, although I keep harriers and not fox-hounds, you are never to touch a fox. You will get me into trouble with all my neighbours. I give you a month's notice. You will leave on this day month."

"Very well, Squire," said Giles, "I'll leave, and I hope you'll find some one to serve you better. Meanwhile I didn't shoot the dratted fox. At least I only shot her after she'd gone and got herself into a trap which I had set for that there Rectory dog what you told me to make off with on the quiet, so that the young lady might never know what become of it and cry and make a fuss as she did about the last. Then seeing that she was finished, with her leg half chewed off, I shot her, or rather I didn't shoot her as well as I should, for the beggar gave a twist as I fired, and now she's bit me right through the hand. I only hopes you won't have to pay my widow for it, Squire, under the Act, as foxes' bites is uncommon poisonous, especially when they've been a-eating of rotten rabbit."

"Dear me!" said the Red-faced Man softening, "dear me, the beast does seem to have bitten you very badly. You must go and be cauterised with a red-hot iron. It is painful but the best thing to do. Meanwhile, suck it, Giles, suck it! I daresay that will draw out the poison, and if it doesn't, thank my stars! I am insured. Look here, a minute or two can make no difference, for if you are poisoned, you are poisoned. Where can we put this brute? I wouldn't have it seen for ten pounds."

"There's an old pollard, Squire, about five yards away down near the fence, which is hollow and handy," said Giles.

"Quite so," he answered, "I know it well. Do you bring the—dog, Giles. Remember, it was a dog, not a fox."

Then they went to the pollard, and as Giles's hand was hurt the Red- faced Man climbed up it, though Giles tried to prevent him.

"Now then, Giles," he said, "give me the fox—I mean the dog, and I will drop it down. Great Heavens! how this tree stinks. Has there been an earth here?"

"Not as I knows of, Squire," said Giles sullenly.

Grampus stretched his hand down into the hollow of the pollard and dragged up a rotting fox by its tail.

"Giles," he said, "you have been killing more foxes and hiding them in this tree. Giles, I dismiss you at once and without a month's wages."

"All right, sir," said Giles, "I'll go, and I prays you'll find some one what will keep your hares which you must have, and your pheasants which you must have, and your partridges which you must have, without killing these varmints of foxes what eats the lot."

The Red-faced Man descended from the tree holding his nose and looked at Giles. Giles sucked his bleeding hand and looked at him.

"Foxes are very destructive animals," said the Red-faced Man to Giles, "especially when one shoots and keeps harriers."

"They are that, sir," said Giles to the Red-faced Man, "as only those know what has to do with them."

"Put the other in, Giles," said the Red-faced man, "and when you have time, throw some soil on to the top of the lot. This place smells horrible. And look you here, Giles," he added in a voice of thunder, "if ever I find you killing a fox upon this property, you will be dismissed at once, as I have often told you before. Do you understand?"

"Yes, Squire, I understand," answered Giles, "and I'll see to the burying of them this same afternoon, if the pain in my hand will suffer it."

"Very well," said the Red-faced Man, "that's done with— except the cubs. As you have killed the vixen you had better stink the cubs out of the earth. I daresay they are old enough to look after themselves— at any rate I hope so. And now, Giles, we must shoot some of these hares when we begin on the partridges next week. There are too many of them, the tenants are complaining, ungrateful beggars as they are, seeing that I keep them for their sport."

At this point I thought that I had heard enough, and slipped away when their backs were turned. For, friend Mahatma, I had just seen a fox shot, and now I knew what shooting meant.

About a week later I knew better still. It came about thus. By that time the turnips I have mentioned, those that grew in the big field, had swelled into fine, large bulbs with leafy tops. We used to eat them at nights, and in the daytime to lie up among them in our snug forms. You know, Mahatma, don't you, that a form is a little hollow which a hare makes in the ground just to fit itself? No hare likes to sleep in another hare's form. Do you understand?"

"Yes," I answered, "I understand. It would be like a man wearing another man's boots."

"I don't know anything about boots Mahatma, except that they are hard things with iron on them which kick one out of one's form if one sits too close. Once that happened to me. Well, my form was under a particularly fine turnip that had some dead leaves beneath the green ones. I chose it because, like the brown earth, they just matched the colour of my back. I was sleeping there quite soundly when my sister came and woke me.

"There are men in the field," she said, her eyes nearly starting out of her head with fear, for she was always very timid.

"I'm off."

"Are you?" I answered. "Well, I think I shall stop here where I shan't be noticed. If we begin jumping over those turnips they will see us."

"We might run down the rows, keeping our ears close to our backs," she remarked.

"No," I said, "there are too many bare patches."

At this moment a gun went 'bang' some way off; and my sister, like a wise hare, scuttled away at full speed for the wood. But I only made myself smaller than usual and lay watching and listening.

There was a good deal to see and hear; for instance, a covey of partridges, troublesome birds that come scratching and fidgeting about when one wants to sleep, were running to and fro in a great state of concern.

"They are after us," said the old cock.

"I remember the same thing last year. Come on, do."

"How can I with all these young ones to look after?" answered the hen. "Why, if once they are scattered I shall never find them again."

"Just as you like, you know best," said the cock. "Goodbye," and away he flew, while his wife and the rest ran to a little distance, scattered and squatted.

Presently, looking back over my shoulders without turning my head, as a hare can, I saw a line of men walking towards me. There was the Red- faced Man whom Giles called Grampus behind his back and Squire to his face. There was Giles himself, with his hurt hand tied up, holding a kind of stick with a slit in it from which hung a lot of dead partridges whose necks were in the slit. One of them was not dead or had come to life again, for it flapped in the stick trying to fly away. He held these in the hand that was tied up, and in the other, oh, horror! was a dead hare bleeding from its nose. It looked uncommonly like my mother, but whether it were or no I couldn't be quite sure. At least from that day neither my sister nor I ever saw her again. I suppose you haven't met her coming up this big white Road, have you, Mahatma?

"No, no," I answered impatiently, "I have already told you that you are the first hare I have ever seen upon the Road. Please get on with your story, or the Lights will change and the Gates be opened before I hear its end."

Just when I saw her I was thinking of running away, but the sight terrified me so much that I could not stir. You see, Mahatma, I really loved my mother as much as a hare can love anything, which is a good deal.

Well, beyond Giles was, who do you think? That dreadful boy, Tom, with a gun in his hand too. Did I say that they all had guns, except Giles and some beater men, only that Tom's was single-barrelled? Then there were others whom I need not describe, stretching to left and right, and worst of all, perhaps, there was Giles's great black dog, a silly-looking beast which always seemed to have its mouth open and its tongue hanging out, and to be wagging a big tail like the fox's, only black and more ragged.

As I watched, up got the old hen partridge and one of her young ones and flew towards me. The Red-faced Man lifted his gun and fired, once, twice, and down came first the mother partridge and then the young one. I forgot to say that Tom fired too at the old partridge, which fell dead quite close to me, leaving a lot of feathers floating in the air. As it fell Tom screeched out—

"I killed that, father."

This made the Red-faced Man very angry.

"You young scoundrel," he said, "how often have I told you not to shoot at my birds under my nose? No sportsman shoots at another man's birds, and as for killing it, you were yards under the thing. If you do it again I will send you home."

"Sorry, father," said Tom, adding in a low voice with a snigger, "I did kill it after all. Dad thinks no one can hit a partridge except himself."

Just then up jumped my father near to Giles, and came leaping in front of the Red-faced Man about twenty yards away from him.

"Mark hare!" shouted Giles, and Grampus, who was still glowering at Tom and had not quite finished pushing the cartridges into his gun, shut it up in a hurry and fired first one barrel and then the other. But my father, who was very cunning, jumped into the air at the first shot and ducked at the second, so that he was missed; at least I suppose that is why he was missed.

Giles grinned and the Red-faced Man said, "Damn!" What does 'damn' mean, Mahatma? It was a very favourite word with the Red-faced Man, but even now I can't quite understand it."

"Nor can I," I answered. "Go on."

"Well, my poor father next ran in front of Tom, who shot too and hit him in the hind legs so that he rolled over and over in the turnips, kicking and screaming. Have you ever heard a hare scream, Mahatma?"

"Yes, yes, it makes a horrid noise like a baby."

"Wiped your eye that time, Dad," cried Tom in an exultant voice.

"I don't know about wiping my eye," answered his father, turning quite purple with rage, "but I wish you would be good enough, Thomas, not to shoot my hares behind, so that they make that beastly row which upsets me" (I think that the Red-faced Man was really kind at the bottom) "and spoils them for the market. If you can't hit a hare in front, miss it like a gentleman."

"As you do, Dad," said Tom, sniggering again. "All right, I'll try."

"Giles," roared Grampus, pretending not to hear, "send your dog and fetch that hare. I can't bear its screeching."

So that great black dog rushed forward and caught my poor father in its big mouth, although he tried to drag himself away on his front paws, and after that I shut my eyes.

Then a lot of partridges got up and there was any amount of banging, though most of them were missed. This made the Red-faced Man angrier than ever. He took off his hat and waved it, bellowing—

"Call back that brute of a dog of yours, Giles. Call it back at once or I'll shoot it."

So Giles called, "Nigger. Come you 'ere, Nigger! Nigg, Nigg, Nigg!"

But Nigger rushed about putting up partridges all over the place while Grampus stamped and shouted and every one missed everything, till at last Tom sat down on the turnips and roared with laughter.

At length, after Giles had beaten Nigger till he broke a stick over him, making him howl terribly, order was restored, and the line having reformed, began to march down on me. For, Mahatma, I was so frightened by what had happened to my father, and I think my mother, that I didn't remember what he, I mean my dead father, had told me, always to run away when there is a chance, as poor hares can only protect themselves by flight.

So as I had lost the chance I thought that I would just sit tight, hoping that they would not see me. Nor indeed would they if it hadn't been for that horrible Tom.

During the confusion the mother partridge which the Red-faced Man had shot had been forgotten by everybody except Tom. Tom, you see, was certain that he had shot it himself, being a very obstinate boy, and was determined to retrieve it as his own.

Now that partridge had fallen within a yard of me, with its beak and claws pointing to the sky, and when the line had passed where we lay Tom lagged behind to look for it. He did not find it then, whether he ever found it afterwards I am sure I don't know. But he found me.

"By Jove! here's a hare," he said, and made a grab at me just as he had done in the furze bush.

Well, I went. Tom shot when I wasn't more than four yards from him, and the whole charge passed like a bullet between my hind legs and struck the ground under my stomach, sending up such a shower of earth and stones that I was knocked right over.

"I've hit it!" yelled Tom, as he crammed another cartridge into his single-barrelled gun.

By the time that it was loaded I was quite thirty yards away and going like the wind. Tom lifted the gun.

"Don't shoot!" roared the Red-faced Man.

"Mind that there boy!" bellowed Giles.

I was running down between two rows of turnips and presently butted into a lad who was bending over, I suppose to pick up a partridge. At any rate his tail—do you call it his tail, Mahatma?"

"That will do," I answered.

"Well, his tail was towards me; it looked very round and shiny. The shot from Tom's gun hit it everywhere. I wish they had all gone into it, but as he was so far away the charge scattered and six of the bullets struck me. Oh! they did hurt. Put your hand on my back, Mahatma, and you will feel the six lumps they made beneath the grey tufts of hair that grew over them, for they are still there."

Forgetting that we were on the Road, I stretched out my hand; but, of course, it went quite through the hare, although I could see the six little grey tufts clearly enough.

"You are foolish, Hare; you don't remember that your body is not here but somewhere else."

"Quite true, Mahatma. If it were here I could not be talking to you, could I? As a matter of fact, I have no body now. It is —oh, never mind where. Still, you can see the grey tufts, can't you? Well, I only hope that those shot hurt that fat boy half as much as they did me. No, I don't mean that I hope it now, I used to hope it.

My goodness! didn't he screech, much worse than my father when his legs were broken. And didn't everybody else roar and shout, and didn't I dance? Off I went right over the fat boy, who had tumbled down, up to the end of the field, then so bewildered was I with shock and the burning pain, back again quite close to them.

But now nobody shot at me because they all thought the boy was killed and were gathered round him looking very solemn. Only I saw that the Red-faced Man had Tom by the neck and was kicking him hard.

After that I saw no more, for I ran five miles before I stopped, and at last lay down in a little swamp near the seashore to which my mother had once taken me. My back was burning like fire, and I tried to cool it in the soft slush.

## 5 The Coursing

Quite a moon went by before I recovered from Tom's shot. At first I thought that I was going to die, for, although luckily none of my bones were broken, the pain in my back was dreadful. When I tried to ease the agony by rubbing against roots it only became worse, for the fur fell off, leaving sores upon which flies settled. I could scarcely eat or sleep, and grew so thin that the bones nearly poked through my pelt. Indeed I wanted very much to die, but could not. On the contrary, by degrees I recovered, till at last I was quite strong again and like other hares, except for the six little grey tufts upon my back and one hole through my right ear.

Now all this while I had lived in the swamp near the sea, but when my strength returned I thought of my old home, to which something seemed to draw me. Also there were no turnips near the swamp, and as the winter came on I found very little to eat there. So one day, or rather one night, I travelled back home.

As it happened the first hare that I met near the big wood was my sister. She was very glad to see me, although she had forgotten how we came to part, and when I spoke of our father and mother these did not seem to interest her. Still from that time forward we lived together more or less till her end came.

One day—this was after we had made our home in the big wood, as hares often do in winter—there was a great disturbance. When we tried to go out to feed at daylight we found little fires burning everywhere, and near to them boys who beat themselves and shouted. So we went back into the wood, where the pheasants were running to and fro in a great state of mind.

Some hours later, when the sun was quite high, men began to march about and scores of shots were fired a long way off, also a wounded cock-pheasant fell near to us and fluttered away, making a queer noise in its throat. It looked very funny stumbling along on one leg with its beak gaping and two of the long feathers in its tail broken.

"I know what this is," I said to my sister. "Let's be gone before they shoot us. I've had enough of being shot."

So off we went, rushing past a boy by his fire, who yelled and threw a stick at us. But as it happened, on the borders of the property of the Red-faced Man there were poachers who knew that hares would come out of the wood on this day of the shooting and had made ready for us by setting wire nooses in the gaps of the hedges through which we ran. I got my foot into one of these but managed to shake it off. My sister was not so lucky, for her head went into another of them. She kicked and tore, but the more she struggled the tighter drew the noose.

I watched her for a little while until one of the poachers ran up with a stick.

Then I went away, as I could not bear to see her beaten to death, and that was the end of my sister. So now I was the only one left alive of our family, except perhaps some younger brothers whom I did not know, though I think it was one of these that afterwards I saw shot quite dead by Giles. He went over and over and lay as still as though he had never moved in all his life. Death seems a very wonderful thing, Mahatma, but I won't ask you what it is because I perceive that you can't answer.

After this nothing happened to me for a long while. Indeed I had the best time of my life and grew very strong and big, yes, the strongest and biggest hare of any that I ever saw, also the swiftest of foot. Twice I was chased by dogs; once by Giles's black beast, Nigger, and once by that of a shepherd. Finding that I could run right away from them without exerting myself at all, I grew to despise dogs. Ah! little did I know then that there are many different breeds of these animals.

One day in mid-winter, as the weather was very mild and open, I was lying on the rough grass field that I have spoken of which borders a flat stretch of moorland. On this moorland in summer grew tall ferns, but now these had died and been broken down by the wind. Suddenly I woke up from my sleep to see a number of men walking and riding towards me.

They were tenants and others who, although the real coursing season had not yet begun in our neighbourhood, had been asked by Grampus to come to try their greyhounds upon his land. Those of them who walked for the most part held two long, lean dogs on a string, while one or two carried dead hares. They were dreadful-looking hares that seemed to have been bitten all over; at least their coats were wet and broken. I shivered at the sight of them, feeling sure that I was going to be put to some new kind of torture.

Besides the men on foot were those on horseback, among whom I recognised the Red-faced Man and my enemy, the dreadful Tom. Most of the others were people called farmers, who seemed very happy and excited and from time to time drank something out of little bottles which they passed to each other. Giles was not there. Now I know that this was because he hated coursing, which killed down hares. Hares, he thought, out to be shot, not coursed.

Whilst I watched, wondering what to do, there was a shout of "There she goes!" and all the long dogs began to pull at their strings. Off the necks of two of them the collars seemed to fall, and away they leapt pursuing a hare. The men on the horses galloped after them, but the men on foot remained where they were.

Now I was afraid to get up and run lest they should loose the other dogs on me, so I lay still, till presently I saw the hare coming back towards me, followed by the two dogs whose noses almost touched its tail. It was exhausted and tried to twist and spring away to the right. But as it did so one of the dogs caught it in its mouth and bit it till it died.

"That was a rotten hare," said Tom, who cantered up just then, "it gave no course at all."

"Yes," puffed Grampus. "Hope the next one will show better sport."

"Hope so too," answered Tom, "especially as it is Jack and Jill's turn to be slipped, and they are the best greyhounds for twenty miles round."

Then the Red-faced Man gave some orders and Jack and Jill were brought forward by the man whose business it was to slip the dogs. One of them was black and one yellow; I think Jack was the black one—a dreadful, sneaking-looking beast with a white tip to its tail, which ended in a sort of curl.

"Forward now," said Grampus, "and go slow. There's sure to be another puss or two in this rough grass."

Next second I was up and away, and before you could count twelve Jack and Jill were after me. I saw them standing on their hind legs straining at the cord. Then the collars fell from them and they leapt forward like the light. My thought was to get back to the wood, which was about a minute's run behind me, but I did not dare to turn and head for it because of the long line of people through which I must pass if I tried to do so. So I ran straight for the moorland, hoping to turn there and reach the wood on its other side, although this meant a long journey.

For a while all went well with me, and having a good start I began to hope that I should outrun these beasts, as I had the shepherd's dog and the retriever. But I did not know Jack and Jill. Just as I reached the borders of the moor I heard the patter of their feet behind me, and looking back saw them coming up, about as far away as I was from Tom when he shot me.

They were running quite close together and behind them galloped the judge and other men. There was a fence here and I bolted through a hole in it. The greyhounds jumped over and for a moment lost sight of me, for I had turned and run down near the side of the fence. But Tom, who had come through a gap, saw me and waved his arm shouting, and next instant Jack and Jill saw me too.

Then as the going was rough by the fence I took to the open moor, always trying, however, to work round to the left in the hope that I might win the shelter of the wood.

On we went like the wind, and now Jack and Jill were quite

close behind me, though before they got there I had managed to circle so that at last my head pointed to the wood, which was more than half a mile away. Their speed was greater than mine, and I knew that I must soon be caught.

At last they were not more than two yards behind, and for the first time I twisted so that they overshot me, which gave me another start. Three times they came up and three times I wrenched or twisted. The wood was not so far away now, but I was almost spent.

What was I to do! What was I to do! I saw a clump of furze to the left, a big clump and thick, and remembered that there was a hare's run through it. I reached it just as Jill was on the top of me, and once more they lost sight of me for a while as they ran round the clump staring and jumping.

When they saw me again on the further side I was thirty yards ahead of them and the wood was perhaps two hundred and fifty yards away. But now I could only run more slowly, for my heart seemed to be bursting, though luckily Jack and Jill were getting tired also. Still they soon came up, and now I must twist every few yards, or be caught in their jaws.

I can't tell you what I felt, Mahatma, and until you have been hunted by greyhounds you will never know. It was horrible. Yet I managed to twist and jump so that always Jack and Jill just missed me. The farmers on the horses laughed to see my desperate leaps and wrenches.

But Tom did worse than laugh. Noting that I was getting quite near the wood, he rode between me and it, trying to turn me into the open, for he wished to see me killed.

"Don't do that! It isn't sportsmanlike," shouted the Red-faced Man. "Give the poor beast a chance."

I don't know whether he obeyed or not, as just then I made my last double, and felt Jill's teeth cut through the fur of my scut and heard them snap. I had dodged Jill, but Jack was right on to me and the wood still twenty yards away.

I could not twist any more, it was just which of us could get there first. I gathered all my remaining strength, for I was mad, mad with terror, and bounded forward.

After me came Jack, I felt his hot breath on my flank. I jumped the ditch, yes, I found power to jump that ditch where there was a rabbit run just by the trunk of a young oak. Jack jumped after me; we must both have been in the air at the same time. But I got through the rabbit run, whereas Jack hit his sharp nose against the trunk of the tree and broke his neck. Yes, he fell dead into the ditch.

I crawled on a few yards to a thick clump and squatted down, for I could not stir another inch. So it came about that I heard them all talking on the other side.

One of them said I was the finest hare he had ever coursed. Others, who had dragged Jack out of the ditch, lamented his death, especially the owner, who vowed that he was worth £50 and abused Tom. Tom, he said, had caused him to be killed—I don't know how, but I suppose because he had ridden forward and tried to turn me. The Red-faced Man also scolded Tom. Then he added—

"Well, I am glad she got off, for she'll give us a good run with the harriers one day. I shall always know that hare again by the white marks on its back; also it is the biggest I have seen for a long while. Come on, my friends, the dog is dead and there's an end of it. At least we have had a good morning's sport, so let's go to the Hall and get some lunch."

The Hare paused for a little, then looked up at me in its comical fashion and asked—

"Did you ever course hares, Mahatma?"

"Not I, thank goodness," I answered.

"Well, what do you think of coursing?"

"I would rather not say," I replied.

"Then I will," said the Hare, with conviction. "I think it horrible."

"Yes, but, Hare, you do not remember the pleasure this sport gives to the men and the dogs; you look at it from an entirely selfish point of view."

"And so would you, Mahatma, if you had felt Jack's hot

breath on your back and Jill's teeth in your tail."

## 6 The Hunting

The Hare sat silent for a time, while I employed myself in watching certain shadows stream past us on the Great White Road. Among them was that of a politician whom I had much admired upon the earth. In this land of Truth I was grieved to observe certain characteristics about him which I had never before suspected. It seemed to me, alas! that in his mundane career he had not been so entirely influenced by a single- hearted desire for the welfare of our country as he had proclaimed and I had believed. I gathered even that his own interests had sometimes inspired his policy.

He went by, leaving, so far as I was concerned, a somewhat painful impression from which I sought relief in the company of the open- souled Hare.

"Well," I said, "I suppose that you died of exhaustion after your coursing experience, and came on here."

"Died of exhaustion, Mahatma, not a bit of it! In three days I was as well as ever, only much more cunning than I had been before. In the night I fed in the fields upon whatever I could get, but in the daytime I always lay up in woods. This I did because I found out the shooting was over, and I knew that greyhounds, which run by sight, would never come into woods.

The weeks went by and the days began to lengthen. Pretty yellow flowers that I had not seen before appeared in the woods, and I ate plenty of them; they have a nice flavour. Then I met another hare and loved her, because she reminded me of my sister. We used to play about together and were very happy. I wonder what she will do now that I am gone."

"Console herself with somebody else," I suggested sarcastically.

"No, she won't do that, Mahatma, because the hounds 'chopped' her just outside the Round Plantation. I mean they caught and ate her. You think that I am contradicting myself, but I am not. I mean I wonder what she will do without me in whatever world she has reached, for I don't see her here. Well, I went to the little Round Plantation because I found that Giles seldom came there and I thought it would be safer, but as it proved I made a great mistake. One day there appeared the Red-faced Man and Tom and the girl, Ella, and a lot of other people mounted on horses, some of them dressed in green coats with ridiculous-looking caps on their heads.

Also with them were I don't know how many spotted dogs whose tails curled over their backs, not like greyhounds whose tails curl between their legs. Outside of the Plantation those dogs caught and ate my future wife, as I have said. It was her own fault, for I had warned her not to go there, but she was a very self-willed character. As it was she never even gave them a run, for they were all round her in a minute. Then they made a kind of cartwheel; their heads were in the centre of this cartwheel and their tails pointed out. In its exact middle was my future wife.

When the wheel broke up there was nothing of her left except her scut, which lay upon the ground.

I had seen so many of such things that I was not so much shocked as you might suppose. After all a fine hare like myself could always get another wife, and as I have told you she was very self-willed.

So I lay still, thinking that those men and dogs would go away.

But what do you think Mahatma? Just as they were going the boy Tom called out—

"I say, Dad, I think we might as well knock through the Round Plantation. Giles tells me that the old speckle-backed buck lies up here."

"Does he?" said Grampus. "Well, if so, that's the hare I want to see, for I know he'd give us a good run. Here, Jerry" (Jerry was the huntsman), "just put the hounds into that place."

So Jerry put the hounds in, making dreadful noises to encourage them, and of course I came out, as I did not wish to share the fate of my future wife.

"That's him!" screeched Tom. "Look at the grey marks on his back."

"Yes, that's he right enough," shouted the Red-faced Man. "Lay them on, Jerry, lay them on; we're in for a rattling run now, I'll warrant."

So they were laid on and I went away as hard as my legs would carry me. Very soon I found that I had left all those curly-tailed dogs a long way behind.

"Ah!" I said to myself proudly, "these beasts are not greyhounds; they are like Giles's retriever and the sheep dog. They'll never see me again. So I looped along saving my breath and heading for a wood which was quite five miles off that I had once visited from the Marsh on the sea-shore where I lay sick, for I was sure they would never follow me there.

You can imagine, then, Mahatma, how surprised I was when I drew near that wood to hear a hideous noise of dogs all barking together behind me, and on looking back, to see those spotted brutes, with their tongues hanging out, coming along quite close to each other and not more than a quarter of a mile away.

Moreover they were coming after me. I was sure of that, for the first of them kept setting its nose to the ground just where I had run, and then lifting up its head to bay. Yes, they were coming on my scent. They could smell me as Giles's curly dog smells the wounded partridges. My heart sank at the thought, but presently I remembered that the wood was quite close, and that there I should certainly give them the slip.

So I went on quite cheerfully, not even running as fast as I could. But fortune was against me, as everything has always been, for I never found a friend. I ran along the side of a hedgerow which went quite up to the wood, not knowing that at the end of it three men were engaged in cutting down an oak tree. You see, Mahatma, they had caught sight of the hunt and stopped from their work, so that I did not hear the sound of their axes upon the tree. Nor, as my head was so near the ground, did I see them until I was right on to them, at which moment also they saw me.

"Here she is!" yelled one of them. "Keep her out of covert or they'll lose her," and he threw out his arms and began to jump about, as did the other two.

I pulled up short within three or four yards of them. Behind were the dogs and the people galloping upon horses and in front were the three men. What was I to do? Now I had stopped exactly in a gateway, for a lane ran alongside the wood. After a moment's pause I bolted through the gateway, thinking that I would get into the wood beyond. But one of the men, who of course wanted to see me killed, was too quick for me and there headed me again.

Then I lost my senses. Instead of running on past him and leaping into the wood, I swung right round and rushed back, still clinging to the hedgerow. Indeed as I went down one side of it the hounds and the hunters came up on the other, so that there were only a few sticks between us, though fortunately the wind was blowing from them to me. Fearing lest they should see me I jumped into the ditch and ran for quite two hundred yards through the mud and water that was gathered there. Then I had to come out of it again as it ended but here was a fall in the ground, so still I was not seen.

Meanwhile the hunt had reached the three men and I heard them all talking together. The end of it was that the men explained which way I had gone, and once more the hounds were laid on to me. In a minute they got to where I had entered the ditch, and there grew confused because my footmarks did not smell in the water. For quite a long time they looked about till at length, taking a wide cast, the hounds found my smell again at the end of the ditch.

During this check I was making the best of my way back towards my own home; indeed had it not been for it I should have been caught and torn to pieces much sooner than I was. Thus it happened that I had covered quite three miles before once more I heard those hounds baying behind me.

This was just as I got on to the moorland, at that edge of it which is about another three miles from the great house called the Hall, which stands on the top of a cliff that slopes down to the beach and the sea.

I had thought of making for the other wood, that in which I had saved myself from the greyhounds when the beast Jack broke its neck against the tree, but it was too far off, and the ground was so open that I did not dare to try.

So I went straight on, heading towards the cliff. Another mile and they viewed me, for I heard Tom yell with delight as he stood up in his stirrups on the black cob he was riding, and waved his cap. Jerry the huntsman also stood up in his stirrups and waved his cap, and the last awful hunt began.

I ran—oh! how I ran. Once when they were nearly on me I managed to check them for a minute in a hollow by getting among some sheep. But they soon found me again, and came after me at full tear not more than a hundred yards behind. In front of me I saw something that looked like walls and bounded towards them with my last strength. My heart was bursting, my eyes and mouth seemed to be full of blood, but the terror of being torn to pieces still gave me power to rush on almost as quickly as though I had just been put off my form. For as I have told you, Mahatma, I am, or rather was, a very strong and swift hare.

I reached the walls; there was an open doorway in them through which I fled, to find myself in a big garden. Two gardeners saw me and shouted loudly. I flew on through some other doors, through a yard, and into a passage where I met a woman carrying a pail, who shrieked and fell on to her back. I jumped over her and got into a big room, where was a long table covered with white on which were all sorts of things that I suppose men eat. Out of that room I went into yet another, where a fat woman with a hooked nose was seated holding something white in front of her. I bolted under the thing on which she was seated and lay there. She saw me come and began to shriek also, and presently a most terrible noise arose outside.

All the spotted dogs were in the house, baying and barking, and everybody was yelling. Then for a minute the dogs stopped their clamour, and I heard a great clatter of things breaking and of teeth crunching and of the Red-faced Man shouting—

"Those cursed brutes are eating the hunt lunch. Get them out, Jerry, you idiot! Get them out! Great heavens! what's the matter with her Ladyship? Is any one murdering her?"

I suppose that they couldn't get them out, or at least when they did they all came into the other room where I was under the seat on which the fat woman was now standing.

"What is it, mother?" I heard Tom say.

"An animal!" she screamed. "An animal under the sofa!"

"All right," he said, "that's only the hare. Here, hounds, out with her, hounds!"

The dogs rushed about, some of them with great lumps of food still in their mouths. But they were confused, and all went into the wrong places. Everything began to fall with dreadful crashes, the fat woman shrieked piercingly, and her shriek was—

"China! Oh! my china-a. John, you wretch! Help! Help! Help!"

To which the Red-faced Man roared in answer—

"Don't be an infernal fool, Eliza-a. I say, don't be such an infernal fool."

Also there were lots of other noises that I cannot remember, except one which a dog made.

This silly dog had thrust its head up the hole over a fire such as the stops make outside the coverts when men are going to shoot, either to hide something or to look for me there. When it came down again because the Red-faced Man kicked it, the dog put its paws into the fire and pulled it all out over the floor. Also it howled very beautifully. Just then another hound, that one which generally led the pack, began to sniff about near me and finally poked its nose under the stuff which hid me.

It jumped back and bayed, whereon I jumped out the other side. Tom made a rush at me and knocked the fat woman off the thing she was standing on, so that she fell among the dogs, which covered her up and began to sniff her all over. Flying from Tom I found myself in front of something filmy, beyond which I saw grass. It looked suspicious, but as nothing in the world could be so bad as Tom, no, not even his dogs, I jumped at it.

There was a crash and a sharp point cut my nose, but I was out upon the grass. Then there were twenty other crashes, and all the hounds were out too, for Tom had cheered them on. I ran to the edge of the lawn and saw a steep slope leading to the sands and the sea. Now I knew what the sea was, for after Tom had shot me in the back I lived by it for a long while, and once swam across a little creek to get to my form, from which it cut me off.

While I ran down that slope fast as my aching legs would

carry me, I made up my mind that I would swim out into the sea and drown there, since it is better to drown than to be torn to pieces. But why are you laughing, friend Mahatma."

"I am not laughing," I said. "In this state, without a body, I have nothing to laugh with. Still you are right, for you see that I should be laughing if I could. Your story of the stout lady and the dogs and the china is very amusing."

"Perhaps, friend, but it did not amuse me. Nothing is amusing when one is going to be eaten alive."

"Of course it isn't," I answered. "Please forgive me and go on."

"Well, I tumbled down that cliff, followed by some of the dogs and Tom and the girl Ella and the huntsman Jerry on foot, and dragged myself across the sands till I came to the lip of the sea.

Just here there was a boat and by it stood Giles the keeper. He had come there to get out of the way of the hunting, which he hated as much as he did the coursing. The sight of him settled me—into the sea I went. The dogs wanted to follow me, but Jerry called and whipped them off.

"I won't have them caught in the current and drowned," he said. "Let the flea-bitten old devil go, she's brought trouble enough already."

"Help me shove off the boat, Giles," shouted Tom. "She shan't beat us; we must have her for the hounds. Come on, Ella."

"Best leave her alone, Master Tom," said Giles. "I think she's an unlucky one, that I do."

Still the end of it was that he helped to float the little boat and got into it with Tom and Ella.

Just after they had pushed off I saw a man running down the steps on the cliff waving his arms while he called out something. But of him they took no heed. I do not think they noticed him. As for me, I swam on.

I could not go very fast because I was so dreadfully tired; also I did not like swimming, and the cold waves broke over my head, making the cut in my nose smart and filling my eyes with something that stung them. I could not see far either, nor did I know where I was going. I knew nothing except I was about to die, and that soon everything would be at an end; men, dogs—everything, yes, even Tom. I wanted things to come to an end. I had suffered so dreadfully, life was so horrible, I was so very tired. I felt that it was better to die and have done.

So I swam on a long way and began to forget things; indeed I thought that I was playing in the big turnip field with my mother and sister. But just as I was sinking exhausted a hand shot down into the water and caught me by the ears, although from below the fingers looked as though they were bending away from me. I saw it coming and tried to sink more quickly, but could not.

"I've got her," said the voice of Tom gleefully. "My! isn't she a beauty? Over nine pounds if she is an ounce. Only just in time, though," he went on, "for, look! she's drowning; her head wobbles as though she were sea-sick. Buck up, pussie, buck up! You mustn't cheat the hounds at last, you know. It wouldn't be sportsmanlike, and they hate dead hares."

Then he held me by my hind legs to drain the water out of me, and afterwards began to blow down my nose, I did not know why.

"Don't do that, Tom," said Ella sharply. "It's nasty."

"Must keep the life in her somehow," answered Tom, and went on blowing.

"Master Tom," interrupted Giles, who was rowing the boat. "I ain't particular, but I wish you'd leave that there hare alone. Somehow I thinks there's bad news in its eye. Who knows? P'raps the little devil feels. Any way, it's a rum one, its swimming out to sea. I never see'd a hunted hare do that afore."

"Bosh!" said Tom, and continued his blowing.

We reached the shore and Tom jumped out of the boat, holding me by the ears. The hounds were all on the beach, most of them lying down, for they were very tired, but the men were standing in a knot at a distance talking earnestly, Tom ran to the hounds, crying out—

"Here she is, my beauties, here she is!" whereon they got up and began to bay. Then he held me above them.

"Master Tom," I heard Jerry's voice say, "for God's sake let that hare go and listen, Master Tom," and the girl Ella, who of a sudden had begun to sob, tried to pull him back.

But he was mad to see me bitten to death and eaten, and until he had done so would attend to no one. He only shouted, "One—two—three! Now, hounds! *Worry, worry, worry!*"

Then he threw me into the air above the red throats and gnashing teeth which leapt up towards me.

The Hare paused, but added, "Did you tell me, friend Mahatma, that you had never been torn to pieces by hounds, 'broken up,' I believe they call it?"

"Yes, I did," I answered, "and what is more I shall be obliged if you will not dwell upon the subject."

## 7 The Coming of the Red-Faced Man

"As you like," said the Hare. "Certainly it was very dreadful. It seemed to last a long time. But I don't mind it so much now, for I feel that it can never happen to me again. At least I hope it can't, for I don't know what I have done to deserve such a fate, any more than I know why it should have happened to me once."

"Something you did in a previous existence, perhaps," I answered. "You see then you may have hunted other creatures so cruelly that at last your turn came to suffer what you had made them suffer. I often think that because of what we have done before we men are also really being hunted by something we cannot see."

"Ah!" exclaimed the Hare, "I never thought of that. I hope it is true, for it makes things seem juster and less wicked. But I say, friend Mahatma, what am I doing here now, where you tell me poor creatures with four feet never, or hardly ever come?"

"I don't know, Hare. I am not wise, to whom it is only granted to visit the Road occasionally to search for some one."

"I understand, Mahatma, but still you must know a great deal or you would not be allowed in such a place before your time, or at any rate you must be able to guess a great deal. So tell me, why do you think that I am here?"

"I can't say, Hare, I can't indeed. Perhaps after the Gates are open and your Guardian has given you to drink of the Cup, you will go to sleep and wake up again as something else."

"To drink of the cup, Mahatma? I don't drink; at least I didn't, though I can't tell what may happen here. But what do you mean about waking up as something else? Please be more plain. As what else?"

"Oh! who can know? Possibly as you are on the human Road you might even become a man some day, though I should not advise you to build on such a hope as that."

"What do you say, Mahatma? A man! One of those two-legged beasts that hunt hares; a thing like Giles and Tom—yes, Tom? Oh! not that—not that! I'd almost rather go through everything again than become a cruel, torturing man."

As it spoke thus the Hare grew so disturbed that it nearly vanished; literally it seemed to melt away till I could only perceive its outline. With a kind of shock I comprehended all the horror that it must feel at such a prospect as I had suggested to it, and really this grasping of the truth hurt my human pride. It had never come home to me before that the circumstances of their lives—and deaths—must cause some creatures to see us in strange lights.

"Oh! I have no doubt I was mistaken," I said hurriedly, "and that your wishes on the point will be respected. I told you that I know nothing."

At these words the Hare became quite visible again.

It sat up and very reflectively began to rub its still shadowy nose with a shadowy paw. I think that it remembered the sting of the salt water in the cut made by the glass of the window through which it had sprung.

Believing that its remarkable story was done, and that presently it would altogether melt away and vanish out of my knowledge, I looked about me. First I looked above the towering Gates to see whether the Lights had yet begun to change. Then as they had not I looked down the Great White Road, following it for miles and miles, until even to my spirit sight it lost itself in the Nowhere.

Presently coming up this Road towards us I saw a man dressed in a green coat, riding-breeches and boots and a peaked cap, who held in his hand a hunting-whip. He was a fine-looking person of middle age, with a pleasant, open countenance, bright blue eyes, and very red cheeks, on which he wore light-coloured whiskers. In short a jovial-looking individual, with whom things had evidently always gone well, one to whom sorrow and disappointment and mental struggle were utter strangers. He, at least, had never known what it is to "endure hardness" in all his life.

Studying his nature as one can do on the Road, I perceived also that in him there was no guile. He was a good-minded, God-fearing man according to his simple lights, who had done many kindnesses and contributed liberally towards the wants of the poor, though as he had been very rich, it had cost him little thus to gratify the natural promptings of his heart.

Moreover he was what Jorsen calls a "young soul," quite young indeed, by which I mean that he had not often walked the Road in previous states of life, as for instance that Eastern woman had done who accosted me before the arrival of the Hare. So to speak his crude nature had scarcely outgrown the primitive human condition in which necessity as well as taste make it customary and pleasant to men to kill; that condition through which almost every boy passes on his way to manhood, I suppose by the working of some secret law of reminiscence.

It was this thought that first led me to connect the new-comer with the Red-faced Man of the Hare's story. It may seem strange that I should have been so dense, but the truth is that it never occurred to me, any more than it had done to the Hare, that such a person would be at all likely to tread the Road for many years to come. I had gathered that he was comparatively young, and although I had argued otherwise with the Hare, had concluded therefore that he would continue to live his happy earth life until old age brought him to a natural end. Hence my obtuseness.

The man was drifting towards me thoughtfully, evidently much bewildered by his new surroundings but not in the least afraid. Indeed there none are afraid; when they glide from their death-beds to the Road they leave fear behind them with the other terrors of our mortal lot.

Presently he became conscious of the presence of the Hare, and thoughts passed through his mind which of course I could read.

"My word!" he said to himself, "things are better than I hoped. There's a hare, and where there are hares there must be hunting and shooting. Oh! if only I had a gun, or the ghost of a gun!"

Then an idea struck him. He lifted his hunting-crop and hurled it at the Hare.

As it was only the shadow of a crop of course it could hurt nothing. Still it went through the shadow of the Hare and caused it to twist round like lightning.

"That was a good shot anyway," he reflected, with a satisfied smile.

By now the Hare had seen him.

"*The Red-faced Man!*" it exclaimed, "Grampus himself!" and it turned to flee away.

"Don't be frightened," I cried, "he can't hurt you; nothing

can hurt you here."

The Hare halted and sat up. "No," it said, "I forgot. But you saw, he tried to. Now, Mahatma, you will understand what a bloodthirsty brute he is. Even after I am dead he has tried to kill me again."

"Well, and why not?" interrupted the Man. "What are hares for except to be killed?"

"There, Mahatma, you hear him. Look at me, Man, who am I?"

So he looked at the Hare and the Hare looked at him. Presently his face grew puzzled.

"By Jingo!" he said slowly, "you are uncommonly like—you *are* that accursed witch of a hare which cost me my life. There are the white marks on your back, and there is the grey splotch on your ear. Oh! if only I had a gun—a real gun!"

"You would shoot me, wouldn't you, or try to?" said the Hare. "Well, you haven't and you can't. You say I cost you your life. What do you mean? It was my life that was sacrificed, not yours."

"Indeed," answered the Man, "I thought you got away. Never saw any more of you after you jumped through the French window. Never had time. The last thing I remember is her Ladyship screaming like a mad cockatoo, yes, and abusing me as though I were a pickpocket, with the drawing-room all on fire. Then something happened, and down I went among the broken china and hit my head against the leg of a table. Next came a kind of whirling blackness and I woke up here."

"A fit or a stroke," I suggested.

"Both, I think, sir. The fit first—I have had 'em before, and the stroke afterwards—against the leg of the table. Anyway they finished me between them, thanks to that little beast."

Then it was that I saw a very strange thing, a hare in a rage. It seemed to go mad, of course I mean spiritually mad. Its eyes flashed fire; it opened its mouth and shut it after the fashion of a suffocating fish. At last it spoke in its own way— I cannot stop to explain in further detail the exact manner of speech or rather of its equivalent upon the Road.

"Man, Man," it exclaimed, "you say that I finished you. But what did you do to me? You shot me. Look at the marks upon my back. You coursed me with your running dogs. You hunted me with your hounds. You dragged me out of the sea into which I swam to escape you by death, and threw me living to the pack," and the Hare stopped exhausted by its own fury.

"Well," replied the Man coolly, "and suppose I, or my people, did, what of it? Why shouldn't I? You were a beast, I was a man with dominion over you. You can read all about that in the Book of Genesis."

"I never heard of the Book of Genesis," said the Hare, "but what does dominion mean? Does this Book of Genesis say that it means the right to torment that which is weaker than the tormentor?"

"All you animals were made for us to eat," commented the Man, avoiding an answer to the direct question.

"Very good," answered the Hare, "let us suppose that we *were* given you to eat. Was it in order to eat me that you came out against me with guns, then with dogs that run by sight, and then with dogs that run by smell?"

"If you were to be killed and eaten, why should you not be

killed in one of these ways, Hare?"

"Why should I be killed in those ways, Man, when others more merciful were to your hand? Indeed, why should I be killed at all? Moreover, if you wished to satisfy your hunger with my body, why at the last was I thrown to the dogs to devour?"

"I don't quite know, Hare. Never looked at the matter in that light before. But—ah! I've got you now," he added triumphantly. "If it hadn't been for me you never would have lived. You see *I* gave you the gift of life. Therefore, instead of grumbling, you should be very much obliged to me. Don't you understand? I preserved hares, so that without me you would never have been a hare. Isn't that right, Mr.— Mr.—I am sorry I have forgotten your name," he added, turning towards me.

"Mahatma," I said.

"Oh! yes, I remember it now—Mr.—ah—Mr. Hatter."

"There is something in the argument," I replied cautiously, "but let us hear our friend's answer."

"Answer—my answer! Well, here it is. What are you, Man, who dare to say that you give life or withhold it? You a Lord of life, *you!* I tell you that I know little, yet I am sure that you or those like you have no more power to create life than the world we have left has to bid the stars to shine. If the life must come, it will come, and if it cannot fulfil itself as a hare, then it will appear as something else. If you say that you create life, I, the poor beast which you tortured, tell you that you are a presumptuous liar."

"You dare to lecture me," said the Man, "me, the heir of all the ages, as the poet called me. Why, you nasty little animal, do you know that I have killed hundreds like you, and," he added, with a sudden afflatus of pride, "thousands of other creatures, such as pheasants, to say nothing of deer and larger game? That has been my principal occupation since I was a boy. I may say that I have lived for sport; got very little else to show for my life, so to speak."

"Oh!" said the Hare, "have you? Well, if I were you, I shouldn't boast about it just now. You see, we are still outside of those Gates. Who knows but that you will find every one of the living things you have amused yourself by slaughtering waiting for you within them, each praying for justice to its Maker and your own?"

"My word!" said the Man, "what a horrible notion; it's like a bad dream."

He reflected a little, then added, "Well, if they do, I've got my answer. I killed them for food; man must live. Millions of pheasants are sold to be eaten every year at a much smaller price than they cost to breed. What do you say to that, Mr. Hatter? Finishes him, I think."

"I'm not arguing," I replied. "Ask the Hare."

"Yes, ask me, Man, and although you are repeating yourself, I'll answer with another question, knowing that here you must tell the truth. Did you really rear us all for food? Was it for this that you kept your keepers, your running dogs and your hunting dogs, that you might kill poor defenceless beasts and birds to fill men's stomachs? If this was so, I have nothing more to say. Indeed, if our deaths or sufferings at their hands really help men in any way, I have nothing more to say. I admit that you are higher and stronger than we are, and have a right to use us for your own advantage, or even to destroy us altogether if we harm you."

The Man pondered, then replied sullenly—

"You know very well that it was not so. I did not rear up pheasants and hares merely to eat them or that others might eat them. Something forces me to tell you that it was in order that I might enjoy myself by showing my skill in shooting them, or to have the pleasure and exercise of hunting them to death. Still," he added defiantly, "I who am a Christian man maintain that my religion perfectly justified me in doing all these things, and that no blame attaches to me on this account."

"Very good," said the Hare, "now we have a clear issue. Friend Mahatma, when those Gates open presently what happens beyond them?"

"I don't know," I answered, "I have never been there; at least not that I can remember."

"Still, friend Mahatma, is it not said that yonder lives some Power which judges righteously and declares what is true and what is false?"

"I have heard so, Hare."

"Very well, Man, I lay my cause before that Power—do you the same. If I am wrong I will go back to earth to be tortured by you and yours again. If, however, I am right, you shall abide the judgment of the Power, and I ask that It will make of you—a hunted hare!"

Now when he heard these awful words—for they were awful —no less, the Red-faced Man grew much disturbed. He hummed and he hawed, and shifted his feet about. At last he said—

"You must admit that while you lived you had a first-class time under my protection. Lots of turnips to eat and so forth."

"A first-class time!" the Hare answered with withering scorn. "What sort of a time would you have had if some one had shot you all over the back and you must creep away to die of pain and starvation? How would you have enjoyed it if, from day to day, you had been forced to live in terror of cunning monsters, who at any hour might appear to hurt you in some new fashion? Do you suppose that animals cannot feel fear, and is continual fear the kind of friend that gives them a 'first-class time'?"

To this last argument the Man seemed able to find no answer.

"Mr. Hare," he said humbly, "we are all fallible. Although I never thought to find myself in the position of having to do so, I will admit that I may possibly have been mistaken in my views and treatment of you and your kind, and indeed of other creatures. If so, I apologise for any, ah—temporary inconvenience I may have caused you. I can do no more."

"Come, Hare," I interposed, "that's handsome; perhaps you might let bygones be bygones."

"Apologise!" exclaimed the Hare. "After all I have suffered I do not think it is enough. At the very least, Mahatma, he should say that he is heartily ashamed and sorry."

"Well, well," said the Man, "it's no use making two bites of a cherry. I am sorry, truly sorry for all the pain and terror I have brought on you. If that won't do let's go up and settle the matter, and if I've been wrong I'll try to bear the consequences like a gentleman. Only, Mr. Hare, I hope that you will not wish to put your case more strongly against me than you need."

"Not I, Man. I know now that you only erred because the truth had not been revealed to you—because you did not understand. All that I will ask, if I can, is that you may be allowed to tell this truth to other men."

"Well, I am glad to say I can't do that, Hare."

"Don't be so sure," I broke in; "it's just the kind of thing which might be decreed—a generation or two hence when the world is fit to listen to you."

But he took no heed, or did not comprehend me, and went on—

"It is an impossibility, and if I did they would think me a lunatic or a snivelling, sentimental humbug. I believe that lots of my old friends would scarcely speak to me again. Why, putting aside the pleasures of sport, if the views you preach were to be accepted, what would become of keepers and beaters and huntsmen and dog-breeders, and of thousands of others who directly or indirectly get their living out of hunting and shooting? Where would game rents be also?"

"I don't know, I am sure," replied the Hare wearily. "I suppose that they would earn their living in some other way, as they must in countries where there is no sport, and that you would have to make up for shooting rents by growing more upon the land. You know that after all we hares and the other game eat a great deal which might be saved if there were not so many of us. But I am not wise, and I have never looked at the question from that point of view. It may seem selfish, but I have to consider myself and the creatures whose cause I plead, for something inside me is telling me now—yes, now—that all of them are speaking through my mouth. It says that is why I am allowed to be here and to talk with you both; for their sakes rather than for my own."

"If you have more to say you had better say it quickly," I interrupted, addressing the Red-faced Man. "I see that the Lights are beginning to change, which means that soon the Road will be closed and the Gates opened."

"I can't remember anything," he answered. "Yes, there is one matter," he added nervously. "I see, Mr. Hare, that you are thinking of my boy Tom, not very kindly I am afraid. As you have been so good as to forgive me I hope that you won't be hard on Tom. He is not at all a bad sort of a lad if a little thoughtless, like many other young people."

"I don't like Tom," said the Hare, with decision. "Tom shot me when you told him not to shoot. Tom shut me up in a filthy place with a yellow rabbit which he forgot to feed, so that it wanted to eat me. Tom tried to cut me off from the wood so that the running dogs might catch me, although you shouted to him that it was not sportsmanlike. Tom dragged me out of the sea and blew down my nostrils to keep me alive. Tom threw me to the hounds, although Giles remonstrated with him and even the huntsman begged him to let me go. I tell you that I don't like Tom."

"Still, Mr. Hare," pleaded the Red-faced Man, "I hope that if it should be in your power when we get through those Gates, that you will be merciful to Tom. I can't think of much to say for him in this hurry, but there, he is my only son and the truth is that I love him. You know he may live—to be different—if you don't bring some misfortune on him."

"Who am I to bring misfortune or to withhold it?" asked the Hare, softening visibly. "Well, I know what love means, for my mother loved me and I loved her in my way. I tell you that when I saw her dead, turned from a beautiful living thing into a stained lump of flesh and fur, I felt dreadful. I understand now that you love Tom as my mother loved me, and, Man, for the sake of your love—not for his sake, mind —I promise you that I won't say anything against Tom if I can help it, or do anything either."

"You're a real good fellow!" exclaimed the Red-faced Man, with evident relief. "Give me your hand. Oh! I forgot, you can't. Hullo! what's up now? Everything seems to be altering."

As he spoke, to my eyes the Lights began to change in earnest. All the sky (I call it sky for clearness) above the mighty Gates became as it were alive with burning tongues of every colour that an artist can conceive. By degrees these fiery tongues or swords shaped themselves into a vast circle which drove back the walls of darkness, and through this circle, guided, guarded by the spirits of dead suns, with odours and with chantings, descended that crowned City of the Mansions before whose glory imagination breaks and even Vision veils her eyes.

It descended, its banners wavering in the winds of prayer; it hung above the Gates, the flowers of all splendours, Heaven's very rose, hung like an opal on the boundless breast of night, and there it stayed.

The Voice in the North called to the Voice in the South; the Voice in the East called to the Voice in the West, and up the Great White Road sped the Angel of the Road, making report as he came that all his multitude were gathered in and for that while the Road was barred.

He passed and in a flash the Gates were burned away. The ashes of them fell upon the heads of those waiting at the Gates, whitening their faces and drying their tears before the Change. They fell upon the Man and the Hare beside me, veiling them as it were and making them silent, but on me they did not fall. Then, from between the Wardens of the Gates, flowed forth the Helpers and the Guardians (save those who already were without comforting the children) seeking their beloved and bearing the Cups of slumber and new birth; then pealed the question—

"Who hath suffered most? Let that one first taste of peace."

Now all the dim hosts surged forward since each outworn soul believed that it had suffered most and was in the bitterest need of peace. But the Helpers and the Guardians gently pressed them back, and again there pealed, no question but a command.

This was the command:—

"Draw near, thou Hare."

Jorsen asked me what happened after this justification of the Hare, which, if I heard aright, appeared to suggest that by the decree of some judge unknown, the woes of such creatures are not unnoted and despised, or left unsolaced. Of course I had to answer him that I could not tell.

Perhaps nothing happened at all. Perhaps all the wonders I seemed to see, even the Road by which souls travel from There to Here and from Here to There, and the Gates that were burned away, and the City of the Mansions that descended, were but signs and symbols of mysteries which as yet we cannot grasp or understand.

Whatever may be the truth as to this matter of my visions, I need hardly add, however, that no one can be more anxious than I am myself to learn in what way the Red-faced Man, speaking on behalf of our dominant race, and the Hare, speaking as an appointed advocate of the subject animal creation, finished their argument in the light of fuller knowledge. Much also do I wonder which of them was proved to be right, a difficult matter whereon I feel quite incompetent to express any views.

But you see at that moment I woke up. The edge of the Road on which I was standing seemed to give way beneath me, and I fell into space as one does in a nightmare. It is a very unpleasant sensation.

I remember noticing afterwards that I could not have been long asleep. When I began to dream I had only just blown out the candle, and when I awoke again there was still a smouldering spark upon its wick.

But, as I have said, in that spirit-land wither I had journeyed is to be found neither time nor space nor any other familiar thing.

Printed in Great Britain
by Amazon

61718552R00054